HIDDEN SCROLLS

BOOK SIX
THE LION'S ROAR

BY M. J. THOMAS

WORTHY
kids™

For my beautiful wife, Lori. Thank you for your love, support, and belief. I couldn't do this without you!

—M.J.T.

ISBN: 978-0-8249-5705-6

WorthyKids
Hachette Book Group
1290 Avenue of the Americas
New York, NY 10104

Library of Congress Cataloging-in-Publication Data
Names: Thomas, M. J., 1969- author. | Reed, Lisa (Illustrator) illustrator.
Title: The lion's roar / M.J. Thomas.
Description: New York, NY : WorthyKids, [2019] | Series: The secret of the hidden
    scrolls ; book six | Summary: Peter, nine, Mary, ten, and their dog, Hank, journey
    into biblical history to Babylon, where they meet Daniel and see Michael, the
    archangel, protect him in the lions' den.
Identifiers: LCCN 2019016580 | ISBN 9780824957056 (pbk. : alk. paper)
Subjects: | CYAC: Time travel—Fiction. | Daniel (Biblical figure—Fiction. | Jews—
    History—953-586 B.C—Fiction. | Brothers and sisters—Fiction. | Dogs—Fiction. |
    Babylonia—Fiction.
Classification: LCC PZ7.1.T4654 Lio 2019 | DDC [Fic]—dc23LC record available at
    https://lccn.loc.gov/2019016580

Cover illustration by Graham Howells
Interior illustrations by Lisa S. Reed
Designed by Georgina Chidlow-Irvin

Lexile® level 430L

Printed and bound in the U.S.A.
CW
10 9 8

CONTENTS

PROLOGUE

Nine-year-old Peter and his ten-year-old sister, Mary, stood at the door to the huge, old house and waved as their parents drove away. Peter and Mary and their dog, Hank, would be spending the month with Great-Uncle Solomon.

Peter thought it would be the most boring month ever—until he realized Great-Uncle Solomon was an archaeologist. Great-Uncle Solomon showed them artifacts and treasures and told them stories about his travels around the globe. And then he shared his most amazing discovery of all—the Legend of the Hidden Scrolls! These weren't just dusty old scrolls. They held secrets—and they would lead to travel through time.

Soon Peter, Mary, and Hank were flung back in time to important moments in the Bible. They witnessed the Creation of the earth. They helped Noah load the animals onto the ark before the flood. They endured the plagues in Egypt. They stood on top of the walls of Jericho as the walls crumbled to the ground. They watched as David battled Goliath. They had exciting adventures, all while trying to solve the secrets in the scrolls.

Now Peter and Mary are ready for their next adventure . . . as soon as they hear the lion's roar.

The Legend of the Hidden Scrolls

THE SCROLLS CONTAIN THE TRUTH YOU SEEK.
BREAK THE SEAL. UNROLL THE SCROLL.
AND YOU WILL SEE THE PAST UNFOLD.
AMAZING ADVENTURES ARE IN STORE
FOR THOSE WHO FOLLOW THE LION'S ROAR!

READY OR NOT

Great-Uncle Solomon sat in his comfy leather chair, covered his eyes, and started counting. "One, two, three."

Peter and Mary ran through the house searching for the perfect place to hide.

"Ruff!" Hank barked as Peter ran past Great-Uncle Solomon.

"That's not fair!" said Peter. "If Hank is on your team, he has to cover his eyes too."

Hank turned and hid his eyes under his paws.

"Four, five, six, seven," counted Great-Uncle Solomon.

Peter and Mary ran toward the shiny suit of armor.

Peter stopped and tried to figure out which way to go. Great-Uncle Solomon's house was huge, and there were lots of places to hide. It was two stories with long hallways leading to room after room filled with all of his archaeological discoveries. Peter thought it was more like a museum than a house.

"Eight, nine," said Great-Uncle Solomon.

"Let's split up," said Mary. "It will be harder to find us."

"Good idea," said Peter. He pointed up the stairs. "You go that way."

Mary hurried up the stairs to find her hiding place.

Peter ran past the suit of armor, down the hallway. He slid to a stop in front of the tall wooden doors to the library. He reached for the handle shaped like a lion's head. He tried to open it, but the handle wouldn't turn.

"I guess I'll have to wait for the lion's roar," he said to himself.

"Ten, eleven, twelve, thirteen," Great-Uncle Solomon's counting echoed down the hallway.

Peter's heart pounded. He only had until the count of twenty to hide. He headed back toward the living room and saw Great-Uncle Solomon and Hank with their heads down.

"Fourteen, fifteen, sixteen, seventeen."

Peter spotted a door underneath the stairs. He opened the door and discovered a closet filled with coats and boxes. He closed the door behind him and scooted some of the boxes over so he could hide in the corner.

One of the boxes fell and spilled onto the floor. Peter felt in the darkness and picked up books and a small flashlight. He turned on the

flashlight to see what else had fallen out. He saw a
compass. *Maybe I can use this on our next adventure,*
thought Peter as he tucked it in his pocket.

"Eighteen, nineteen, twenty," counted Great-
Uncle Solomon. "Ready or not, here I come!"

"*Woof!*" Hank barked.

Peter turned off the flashlight and crouched
quietly in the corner behind the boxes. He heard
footsteps coming toward the door. He held his
breath and didn't move a muscle.

The footsteps walked past the door. Peter could hear them walking up the stairs—right above his head. He let out a sigh of relief. Then the footsteps stopped.

"Aarf, aarf!" barked Hank.

"What is it, Hank?" said Great-Uncle Solomon.

Peter heard Hank's paws coming down the stairs, around the corner, and then scratching at the closet door.

Great-Uncle Solomon swung the door wide open. Light flooded into the dark closet. Hank found Peter crouched in the corner and licked his face.

Peter stood up and wiped off the slobber. "How did you find me?"

Great-Uncle Solomon petted Hank's head. "Hank is good at hide-and-seek! Now let's go find Mary."

They left the closet and headed past the shiny

suit of armor. Hank stopped and made a low growl at the armor.

Great-Uncle Solomon peeked around the armor. "She's not hiding there."

Peter stared at the knight. "Where did you find the armor?"

Great-Uncle Solomon rubbed his chin. "I was on an archaeology expedition in Rome," he said. "I discovered a long, dark tunnel that led to ancient catacombs."

"What are catacombs?" said Peter.

"They are man-made caves where very important people were buried."

A shiver ran through Peter's body. "Like an underground cemetery?"

Great-Uncle Solomon adjusted his round glasses under his bushy, white eyebrows. "Exactly."

"Who did the armor belong too?" asked Peter.

"I believe it belonged to . . . "

"*Ahhhhh!*" A high-pitched scream came from upstairs.

A Pile of Tiles

"That's Mary!" said Peter. "Let's go see what happened!"

"*Ahhhhh!*" Mary screamed again.

"Hank!" said Peter. "Find Mary!"

Hank darted up the stairs with Peter and Great-Uncle Solomon on his trail. Peter was surprised how quickly Great-Uncle Solomon moved. He was so old.

Hank took a sharp left at the top of the stairs and headed down the long hallway. He ran back and forth sniffing one door after another.

"*Ruff!*" Hank scratched at the fourth door on the left.

When Peter caught up with Hank, he pressed his ear against the door. He didn't hear a sound. "Are you sure she's in there?"

"*Woof!*" Hank barked and wagged his tail.

Peter tuned the knob and slowly opened the door to a dark room. He shined his flashlight around the room and saw Mary standing in the middle with her back to them. She was frozen like a popsicle.

"We found you!" shouted Peter.

"Shhh," said Mary, slowly walking backward.

"What's wrong?" whispered Great-Uncle Solomon.

"There's a lion on the other side of the room," she whispered.

Hank ran into the room and growled.

"Stop, Hank!" said Mary. "It's too big."

Peter shined the light across the room as Mary ran out.

"Do you see it?" said Mary.

Peter laughed. "I found your scary lion."

"Then why are you laughing?" said Mary.

Great-Uncle Solomon reached in the room and turned on the light. "It's not alive," he said. "It's just a statue."

Mary's cheeks turned red. "Well, it looked real in the dark."

Peter walked over to the lion and ran his hand across the rough stone lion's mane. Its mouth was wide open, revealing massive fangs.

"It is a little scary," said Peter, holding back his laughter.

Mary walked over to the lion. "Where did you discover it?"

Great Uncle-Solomon stared at the lion for a moment. "On an archaeology dig many, many years ago."

"Before we were born?" asked Mary.

Great-Uncle Solomon chuckled. "Yes, it was before your parents were born."

"Wow!" said Peter. "That was a long time ago."

"Where was the dig?" said Mary.

Great-Uncle Solomon walked quickly across the room to a huge table covered in dusty artifacts. "Where's that map?" he muttered. "Oh, here it is." He unrolled an old map on the table.

Hank stood on his hind legs and put his paws on the table. Peter and Mary crowded in for a closer look.

"This is a map of ancient Babylon," he said.

Peter looked at the map and saw a huge city

surrounded by a wall. There was a large palace, lots of temples, and a long river running straight through the middle.

Great-Uncle Solomon pointed to a blue circle near a temple. "I found it right here."

Mary pointed at a big red X beside a long road leading to the palace. "What happened here?"

Great-Uncle Solomon thought for a moment. "Oh yes, I remember." He rolled up the map and handed it to Peter. "Keep this. You might need it."

"Why would I need an old map?" Peter asked.

"For your next adventure, of course," said Great-Uncle Solomon.

Peter's shoulders slumped. "I don't know if there will be another adventure," he said. "It's been four days since the lion roared and we traveled back in time."

Great-Uncle Solomon put his hand on Peter's shoulder. "I know it's hard to wait," he said. "But remember that God has a plan."

"So what was the red X for?" interrupted Mary.

"Oh yes, the red X," he said. He led them to a large wooden table piled with stacks of tiles. "That is where I found these."

Peter picked up a few of the rectangular tiles. Some were blue. Some were yellow. Some were blue and yellow.

"I think these are important," said Great-Uncle Solomon. "I just can't figure out what they are."

"Mary is good at solving problems," said Peter. "Maybe she can figure it out."

"Well, what do you think it could be?" said Great-Uncle Solomon.

Mary looked at the piles of tiles. She grabbed some of the colorful tiles and spread them out on the table. "Maybe it's some kind of puzzle."

She started to slide the tiles around the table, matching blue with blue and yellow with yellow.

"I think you're right," said Great-Uncle Solomon. "Why couldn't I see it before?"

Mary slid a tile to the bottom of the puzzle.

"That looks like two legs!" said Peter. Then he picked up a tile. "This looks like the end of a tail."

Mary took the tile and slid it into place.

"You're right," said Great-Uncle Solomon.

Peter folded his arms and grinned. "Glad I could help."

"That's all the pieces," said Mary.

They studied the finished puzzle. It was missing a section in the top right corner—right where the head should be.

"It looks like some kind of animal," said Peter.

"Of course, it's an animal," said Mary. "It has four legs and a tail."

Peter shrugged his shoulders. "I was just trying to help."

Great-Uncle Solomon folded his arms and

stared at the puzzle. "Yes, Peter is right . . . it is definitely an animal."

Mary sighed. "I know it's an animal," she said. "But what kind of animal?"

"It's hard to say without the head," said Great-Uncle Solomon.

Peter was getting bored with the puzzle. He turned and noticed Hank in the middle of the room, sitting very still and staring at the lion.

"*Grrrrr.*" Hank made a low growl.

Peter walked over the to the large stone lion. "It's not real," he said to Hank. He slowly reached his hand toward the open mouth of the lion. He stretched out his finger to touch one of the long, sharp fangs.

Roar!

"Ahhhh!" Peter jumped back from the lion.

Mary laughed. "That wasn't the statue," she said. "That roar came from the library downstairs."

Peter's heart was racing. "I know," he said. "I was just kidding."

Mary put her hands on her hips. "Sure you were," she said.

Roar! The call of the lion echoed through the house again.

"Hurry!" said Great-Uncle Solomon. "It's time for your next adventure, and you don't want to keep the lion waiting."

"Let's go!" said Peter.

Peter, Mary, and Hank darted out of the room, down the stairs, past the shiny suit of armor, and down the hallway.

Peter stopped at his bedroom and grabbed his brown, leather adventure bag. He shoved the map, compass, and flashlight into the bag and headed to the library. Mary and Hank were waiting for him at the door.

Peter looked up at the tall wooden doors that reminded him of a castle. He reached for the handle shaped like a lion's head and twisted.

Click!

Peter swung the door open, and they all ran in. The door slammed behind them.

Roar! The sound came from behind the tall bookshelf on the right. Hank ran over and barked at one of the books.

Mary found the red book with a lion's head

painted in gold on the cover. She pulled it from the shelf. The tall bookshelf rumbled and slid open to reveal a hidden room. It was dark except for a glowing clay pot in the center of the room holding the Hidden Scrolls.

Hank ran in and barked at one of the scrolls.

Peter pulled out the scroll that Hank was so interested in.

"What's on the red wax seal?" said Mary.

"It looks like a lion," said Peter.

"I think I'm starting to see a pattern," said Mary.

"What do you mean?" said Peter.

Mary shook her head. "All of the lions around here!" she blurted out.

"I guess you're right," Peter said. "I wonder what it means?"

"I don't know," Mary said. "Open the scroll and let's find out."

Peter broke the seal. Suddenly, the walls shook, books fell from the shelves, and the floor quaked.

Peter grabbed Mary's hand. "Here we go!"

The library crumbled around them and disappeared. Then everything was still and quiet.

WELCOME TO BABYLON

Peter slipped the scroll into the adventure bag and looked around. They stood in the middle of a room with high ceilings and a floor made of large, smooth stones. There was one large window and two doors.

"Where do you think we are?" said Peter.

"I don't know," said Mary. She walked over to the one of the walls and looked closely. Blue tiles shimmered in the sunlight streaming through the window. "These look just like the tiles Great-Uncle Solomon discovered!"

Peter rubbed his hand over the wall. "You're right," he said.

He walked over to the window and gasped. "Whoa! We are really high!" Peter held tight to the windowsill. He didn't want to fall out!

"*Ruff!*" Hank put his paws on the windowsill so he could see too.

Peter grabbed his collar. "Be careful, Hank," he said. "That's a long way down."

Mary ran over and stuck her head out of the window. "I think I know where we are."

"On top of a pyramid?" asked Peter.

"Close, but not exactly," said Mary. "We're in a ziggurat."

Peter scratched his head. "A zig-your-what?"

"No," said Mary. "It's a ziggurat. It's like a pyramid, except it's built in layers."

Peter raised his eyebrows. "So, like I said— a pyramid."

Mary just shook her head. "Do you have the map Great-Uncle Solomon gave us?"

Peter reached into his bag. "Here you go."

Mary unrolled the map and looked out the window. "Just like I thought," she said. "We've traveled back in time to ancient Babylon."

"Are you sure?" said Peter.

Mary pointed at the ziggurat on the map. "We are here," she said. She ran her finger along the river on the map. "And that is the Euphrates River."

Peter looked at the map, then looked out of the window. "It does look similar."

Mary pointed to the top of the map. "And there is the palace."

Peter carefully stuck his head out the window again and looked to the right. He saw a large palace in the distance. It was surrounded by palm trees and protected by a large gate covered in blue tiles. Peter thought the tiles almost looked like water against the desert that surrounded the huge city.

Peter looked back at the map. "I think you're right," he said. "We're in ancient Babylon."

"Ruff!" Hank barked and ran to a door on the other side of the room.

Peter and Mary ran over to join him. Hank scratched at the tall, bronze door with a red dragon painted on it. The dragon had large wings and the head of a snake.

Peter shook his head. "Why are there always snakes?"

Hank growled and scratched at the door again.

"Let's see what's inside," said Peter.

Mary backed away. "I don't have a good feeling about this."

She pointed to the other door. "Let's go out that door and get out of here."

Hank kept scratching at the dragon door.

"Come on, Mary," said Peter. "Who knows?

We might find a clue that can help us solve the secret in the scroll."

Mary took a deep breath. "Okay, go ahead and open the door."

Peter slowly reached for the handle that was shaped like a dragon's claw and pulled the door open. Mary stayed behind him as they walked through the doorway. Tall candle holders surrounded the room. The flickering light reflected on the walls.

Hank ran across the room and growled.

Peter followed Hank, then stopped in the middle of the room. "Maybe we shouldn't have come in here."

"What's wrong?" said Mary, running over to join him.

"Look!" Peter pointed at a tall statue of a man with a long beard and a cup-shaped hat. The man had a long red robe with golden stars. "That

statue is taller than Goliath!"
said Peter.

"*Shhh,*" said Mary. "We
better get out of here before
someone finds us."

"Yeah," whispered
Peter. "I'm getting the
creeps."

Hank just kept growling
at the statue.

Peter let out a low whistle.
"Come on, Hank."

Then a whistle came from
the statue.

Mary's eyes got as big as
coconuts. "What was that?"

"*Bow!*" said a scratchy voice from
the statue. "*Bow!*" the voice repeated.

"Is the statue talking?" asked Peter.

28

"*Ruff!*" Hank barked at the statue.

A large black raven peeked its head over the top of the hat on the statue. "*Bow!*" squawked the raven, spreading its wings.

"I didn't know ravens could talk," said Peter.

"They can," said Mary. "Just like a parrot."

"Well," said Peter, "you learn something new every day."

The raven flew over their heads and out the dragon door.

"Now let's get out of here," said Mary.

They turned and walked toward the door. Peter stopped in his tracks as a shadow crept through the door followed by a man with a long beard. He was dressed just like the statue. The raven was perched on his shoulder.

"*Bow!*" squawked the raven.

"Good job!" said the man. He reached into his pocket and fed the raven some seeds.

Peter backed slowly into the room, with Mary behind him. Hank stood in front of them and growled.

"Well, well, what do we have here?" said the man. "We don't have visitors in the temple very often."

Peter looked at the man. Then he looked at the statue. "Is that statue of you?"

The man laughed and the raven crowed.

"Silence!" said the man with a stern look at the raven. He turned back to Peter. "That is not a statue, my young boy. That is the great god, Marduk!"

"Then who are you?" asked Mary.

The man scowled at her. "I am the High Priest of Babylon!" He walked around them and stood in front of the towering statue.

"Bow!" squawked the raven.

"Yes, my little feathered friend," said the High

Priest. He stroked the raven's head then glared at Peter and Mary. "Bow before the great Marduk!"

Peter stood upright. "No, we will not bow to an idol."

The High Priest pointed and lowered his voice. "I said, 'Bow!'"

Peter and Mary wouldn't bow.

"No, we only worship the one true God," said Peter. He felt the scroll shake in the adventure bag. He held it tight so the High Priest wouldn't notice.

Peter turned and grabbed Mary's arm. "I think we'll be leaving now."

The raven flew out of the room. The High Priest darted around them and blocked the door. Peter was surprised at how quickly he moved.

"I will give you one more chance," snapped the High Priest. "Bow! Or you will be thrown into the dungeon."

"We won't bow to your idol," said Mary.

"Bad decision," said the High Priest. "Guards!"

The raven flew through the door followed by five guards carrying ropes.

"Take them to the dungeon!" said the High Priest.

Hank stood in front of Peter and Mary and growled. One of the guards threw a net over Hank, and the others surrounded Peter and Mary.

"This isn't going well," whispered Peter as a guard tied his trembling hands behind his back.

"Help!" shouted Mary.

"Silence!" said the High Priest. "No one is going to help you."

Run!

"God will help us!" said Peter. He felt his bag shake again.

"Marduk will not help you," said the High Priest.

"I'm not talking about your fake god," said Peter. "I'm talking about the real God." Peter squeezed the shaking bag under his arm.

The High Priest looked down at the bag. "What are you hiding in your bag?" He stepped toward Peter. "Did you steal something from the temple?"

Peter took a step back. "No, I didn't steal anything."

"I'll take a look for myself!" The High Priest reached for the adventure bag.

"Help!" Peter shouted.

Just then, a mighty wind rushed through the dragon door. The wind swirled through the room, blowing out candles and sending the guards sliding across the floor. The raven tried to fly away, but the wind was too strong.

The High Priest backed away from Peter and Mary. He watched the swirling wind as it whipped around the room. Peter thought it looked like a little tornado.

The swirling stopped. The angel Michael stood in the middle of the room with his mighty wings spread wide.

The guards ran to hide behind the idol. The raven perched on the High Priest's shoulder.

"I'm not afraid of you," snarled the High Priest.

Michael drew his flaming sword and filled the room with light.

"You should be!" said Peter.

The High Priest took a few steps back.

Michael swung his sword, and the ropes fell from Peter and Mary's wrists. He swung again, and the net fell off Hank. Peter rubbed his arms, surprised that the sword hadn't hurt at all.

"Run!" shouted Michael.

Peter, Mary, and Hank ran out of the door as fast as their feet and paws could carry them.

"Let's go that way!" said Mary, pointing toward the other door in the main room.

As Mary pulled the door open, Peter heard the dragon door slam behind them. He turned and saw Michael holding the door shut.

"Run and hide in the garden," said Michael. "I'll slow them down."

"Where's the garden?" asked Peter.

Bang! The door shook behind Michael.

"Go to the garden—now!" said Michael. "I'll find you there."

Peter stepped outside the door. The sunlight hit his face. He shaded his eyes and looked at the hundreds of steps leading down the side of the ziggurat. Peter turned back around to Mary and Hank. "Let's go!"

Down they went—step after step—level after level. Peter was out of breath when they finally reached the bottom. Mary put her hands on her knees and took a deep breath. Peter looked to the top of the ziggurat and saw Michael flying away. Then he saw the High Priest standing at the top of the steps and looking down at them.

"Guards, get them!" he shouted.

Peter looked around—the courtyard was surrounded by tall walls. He looked up and saw the guards coming down the stairs with the raven flying over their heads.

He spotted an open gate. "That way!" Peter said as he took off running.

"You can run!" the High Priest shouted from the top of the ziggurat. "But you cannot hide!"

With Hank in the lead, they made it through

the gate before the guards could make it down the stone steps.

"Ruff!" Hank barked at the raven flying straight at them.

Peter grabbed the gate and swung it shut.

Clunk! The raven flew right into it.

"That should keep him quiet for a while," said Peter. He turned and saw a wide street filled with people wearing colorful robes. The street was lined with walls covered in blue and yellow tiles.

"Which way should we go?" said Peter.

"Let's go this way," said Mary. She slipped into the crowd of people.

Peter shoved his way into the crowd behind Mary. Hank stayed right by his leg. "Why are they all in such a hurry?" Peter said as people flowed around them.

"Just keep walking with the crowd," said Mary. "The guards won't be able to find us."

The crowd rushed down the street like a river. Mary pointed to a small road through an arched passageway on the right side of the street. "Let's go that way."

They nudged their way through the crowd and through the arch. The smaller road was lined with small, square houses made of sand-colored bricks.

Peter pointed to a tall wall ahead of them. "Maybe the garden is in there."

As they rounded a corner, Peter found a gate.

"Grrrrr," Hank made a low growl at the statue of a lion standing guard at the gate.

A chill ran through Peter. "That looks just like the statue at Great-Uncle Solomon's house!"

Mary stepped closer to the statue and looked into its eyes. "It's definitely the same lion," said Mary. "I would recognize those eyes anywhere."

Peter looked through the gate and saw a large building decorated with colorful tiles and a golden star. "It's not the garden," said Peter. "It looks like another temple."

Mary snapped her fingers. "I know how we can find the garden!" she said. "Let's look at the map."

Peter pulled the map out of his bag.

"Great-Uncle Solomon marked the spot where he found the lion!" said Mary.

"Oh yeah," said Peter. "But how does that help us find the garden?"

Mary pointed to the blue circle on the map. "It means we are right here next to the Ishtar Temple."

"I get it," said Peter. "If we can find the garden on the map, we can figure out how to get there."

"Exactly!" said Mary.

Peter and Mary studied the map.

"There it is!" said Peter, pointing at the map. "The Hanging Gardens."

"So we just need to go northwest and we'll find it," said Mary.

Peter looked around. "But which way is northwest?"

Mary scratched her head. "I'm not sure."

"I almost forgot." said Peter. He stuck his hand in the adventure bag. "I have a compass!"

THE HANGING GARDENS

Peter held up the compass, and Mary read the map. They made their way through a maze of narrow streets, then across a wider road named Processional Way on the map. The route led to the corner of the palace.

Peter looked at a towering garden filled with palm trees, plants, and colorful flowers. "I think we found the garden."

Mary looked around. "The coast is clear."

They snuck through the gate and made their way into the garden.

Hank chased a butterfly in circles.

Mary stopped to smell purple flowers growing from a vine climbing a brick wall. "These smell wonderful," she said. "No wonder they called this garden one of the Seven Wonders of the Ancient World."

"What are the seven wonders?" asked Peter.

"They were the most amazing places in the ancient world," said Mary. "They included the Pyramids of Giza and the Hanging Gardens of Babylon."

Peter looked around and shrugged. "I guess it's nice . . . if you like flowers."

Hank chased a lizard across the path.

"*Ahhhhh!*" Mary screamed and jumped.

Peter picked up the little lizard and held it in front of Mary.

She quickly dropped into a karate pose. "Put it down!"

"Okay, okay," said Peter. He put the lizard in a bush.

"We need to stop playing around and find Michael," said Mary.

They searched high and low in the garden but couldn't find Michael anywhere. The sun began to set behind the tall palm trees.

"I guess we'll sleep here and wait for Michael," said Peter.

Peter found a good spot under a palm tree, and they settled in. Peter rested his head on the adventure bag and gazed into the starry sky.

The palm branches above him started shaking. Hank barked and Mary sat up.

"What was that?" she whispered.

Peter looked up at the palm branches. "I hope it's not the raven," he whispered back.

A strong gust of wind blew, and the tree swayed.

"Maybe it was just the wind," said Mary.

"*Grrrrr,*" Hank growled at some tall bushes a few feet away.

Peter grabbed his collar. "Hank, stay!"

The bushes rustled and bent.

Peter's heart thumped. "I don't think that was the wind."

Michael poked his head through the bushes. "There you are!"

Peter took a deep breath. "You scared us!"

"Sorry," said Michael. "I didn't mean to sneak up on you."

"It's okay," said Mary. "I'm glad you found us."

"What took you so long?" asked Peter.

"Babylon is a huge city," said Michael, "and the enemy, Satan, is causing many problems."

"What kind of problems?" said Mary.

"He is deceiving the people," said Michael, "and causing them to worship false gods and idols."

"There do seem to be a lot of temples and idols in Babylon," said Peter.

"Yes," said Michael. "The enemy wants to stop people from believing in the one true God. Now, let's go over the rules of your adventure."

Michael held up one finger. "First rule: you have to solve the secret in the scroll in four days or you will be stuck here."

Peter thought about his parents. It had been a long time since he had seen them. "We need to solve it so we can get back to Great-Uncle Solomon's house. We have to be there when our parents get home from their trip."

Hank leaned into Peter's leg.

Mary put her hand on Peter's shoulder. "We can solve it," she said. "We'll see them again."

Michael held up two fingers. "Second rule: you can't tell anyone where you are from or that you are from the future."

Peter and Mary nodded.

Michael held up three fingers. "Third rule: you can't try to change the past. Now let's look at the scroll."

"Peter, didn't the scroll shake while we were in the temple?" said Mary.

"Oh yeah," said Peter. "And it shakes when we solve one of the words." Peter reached into the bag and pulled out the scroll. He unrolled it and saw four words written in strange symbols. The first word glowed and transformed into the word: GOD.

Peter and Mary gave each other a high-five.

"We solved the first word!" said Peter.

Peter looked back at the strange symbols on the scroll.

Mary looked over Peter's shoulder. "It looks like the secret is written in cuneiform," she said.

"It looks like chicken scratch to me," said Peter.

"Cuneiform is one of the most ancient forms of writing," said Mary, like everyone should know that.

"Very impressive," said Michael.

Peter rolled his eyes. "I still think it looks like chicken scratch," he said. "Do you know what it says?"

Mary studied the scroll for a little while then sighed, "No, I can't figure it out."

"Don't worry," said Michael. "You're off to a really good start. You only have three words left to solve."

Peter stretched and let out a big yawn.

"Get some sleep," said Michael. "You have a big adventure ahead." Then he spread his mighty wings. "I must go. Remember to be on guard against the enemy, Satan." Michael flapped his wings and flew into the star-filled sky.

Peter put the scroll back in the adventure bag. They settled down under a flower bush and drifted off to sleep.

A NEW FRIEND

Peter woke to water dripping on his face. He wiped it off. Then more water splashed on his head. *"Ugh!"* Peter grunted. He scooted from under the flower bush.

"Ahhhhh!" A young girl standing in the garden screamed. Peter thought she looked about the same age as Mary. She wore a long, white robe and was watering the flowers with a large clay pot.

"Don't be afraid," said Peter.

Mary scooted out and brushed water from

her forehead. Hank crawled out next and shook. Water flew everywhere.

The young girl giggled. "My name is Hannah," she said. She had brown wavy hair. Her brown eyes sparkled, and her warm smile made Peter feel safe.

"My name is Peter," he said. "This is my sister, Mary, and my dog, Hank."

"It's nice to meet you," said Hannah. She looked at their clothes. "You don't look like you're from around here."

"We're not," said Mary. "We've come on a long journey."

"Are you from Nineveh?" Hannah asked.

"No," said Peter. "Much further."

"Well then, you have come on a long journey," she said. "Why were you sleeping under the flower bush?"

"We're hiding," said Peter.

Hannah looked around. "Who are you hiding from?" she whispered.

"The High Priest of Babylon," said Mary.

"And his annoying raven," added Peter.

"He *is* trouble," said Hannah. "He tries to control Babylon and make everyone worship his fake gods."

"Yeah," said Peter. "He tried to make us bow to Marduk."

Hannah got a serious look on her face. "Did you bow?"

"No," said Peter. "We believe in the one true God. We only bow to him."

Hannah smiled. "Good. I do too," she said. "I'm an Israelite."

"Why are you in Babylon?" said Mary.

"Many years ago, King Nebuchadnezzar defeated Israel and destroyed our beautiful Temple." Hannah sighed and sadness filled her eyes. "King Nebuchadnezzar took my grandfather and many other Israelites captive and made them live here in Babylon."

"Why are you watering the flowers?" asked Peter.

"I work in the garden," said Hannah.

"Is it hard?" asked Mary.

"It's not too bad," said Hannah. "But my family would love to go back to Israel."

Mary sighed. "We know how hard it is to be away from your home."

"Ruff!" Hank barked at a bird flying over the palm trees.

"Was that the raven?" said Mary.

"I don't know," said Peter. "I didn't get a good enough look."

"Follow me," said Hannah. "I can take you to a safe place to hide."

Mary leaned in close to Peter. "Do you think we can trust her?"

Peter looked into Hannah's eyes. "I think so" he said. "Let's go."

They ran out of the garden and made their way to the wide street, which was full of people.

"Where are we going?" asked Peter.

"To my house," said Hannah. "It's on the other end of Processional Way."

"I hope the guards don't see us," said Peter.

They dodged and darted through the crowd. They ducked as they walked past the ziggurat.

"We're almost there," said Hannah.
Something on the blue wall that ran along the street caught Peter's attention.

"Mary, look!" he said, heading over to the wall. Peter looked at the yellow tiles in the wall making the pattern of an animal. He looked at the face of the animal. "It's a lion!"

Hannah shrugged. "Of course it's a lion. What else would it be?"

Peter looked down, embarrassed. "I know it's a lion," he said. "I mean it's just like the lion at Great-Uncle Solomon's house."

Now Hannah looked very confused. "Your uncle has a lion in his house?"

Mary gave Peter *the look*. "Peter gets confused sometimes," she said.

"Ruff!" Hank barked at something across the street.

Peter spun around and spotted the raven perched on top of the wall.

"Bow!" it squawked. Then it flew straight at them.

"Duck!" shouted Peter.

They ducked just in time. The raven flew over their heads and slammed into the face of the lion on the wall. The bird hit with such a mighty thud that it knocked a few tiles off the wall.

Peter picked up the fallen tiles and tried to fit them back on the wall, but they wouldn't stick. So he slipped them in his bag hoping no one would notice what had happened.

The raven stood and shook his head. Then he spread his wings and flew away.

"That was close," said Mary.

"Let's get to my house before he comes back," said Hannah.

Peter turned and looked across the street. "Too late."

The raven was perched on the shoulder of the High Priest.

GALLOP THROUGH BABYLON

"They found us!" said Peter.

Hank crouched in front of Peter, Mary, and Hannah and growled.

Peter quickly looked around. He saw a red chariot ahead of them on the street. It had two big wheels and an open carriage. A white horse was harnessed to the front, and the carriage was empty.

The High Priest walked toward them.

"I have a plan," said Peter. He pointed at the chariot. "Let's go!"

Peter, Mary, and Hannah ran and jumped into the carriage. Hank stayed where he was and barked at the High Priest.

Peter looked around the front of the chariot. "How do you drive this thing?"

"I'll do it!" said Mary. She grabbed the reins and snapped them. *"Heeyah!"*

The horse reared up and took off like a lightning bolt.

"Look out!" shouted Peter.

People scurried out of the way on the street in front of them.

Peter looked back to the street behind them. "Hank, come!" Peter squatted down as Hank ran toward the chariot. He held out his arms and shouted, "Hank, jump!"

Hank leapt into the air—right into Peter's

arms. The chariot wheels rumbled down the cobbled stone street.

"We're losing them!" said Hannah. "But we're going the wrong way!"

Mary pulled back on the reins. *"Whoa!"*

The horse skidded to a stop. Peter, Hannah, and Hank tumbled to the front of the carriage.

"Where did you learn to drive a chariot?" said Peter.

"I read about it in a book," said Mary. *"Real Horse Power: How to Be a Charioteer."*

Peter shook his head. "You read too much."

"Oh no!" said Hannah.

Peter looked back and saw the High Priest and the raven riding a chariot straight at them.

"That guy doesn't give up," said Peter.

"Neither do we!" said Mary. *"Heeyah!"*

The horse bolted down the street.

"They're gaining on us!" said Hannah.

The High Priest's chariot was right behind them. Peter could hear the horse huffing and puffing.

"Faster!" shouted Peter.

"I'm trying!" said Mary. "Where should I go?"

"Go straight to the Ishtar Gate!" said Hannah, pointing ahead. "We can escape Babylon through the gate."

Up ahead, Peter saw a huge blue gate decorated with golden dragons and bulls. He looked back. The High Priest was pulling up on their left side. Peter looked into his cold, dark eyes.

"Shut the gate!" shouted the High Priest.

Soldiers started swinging the huge bronze gate shut.

"What do I do?" said Mary.

"Keep going!" said Hannah.

"But the gates are closing!" said Mary.

"Trust me," said Hannah.

Mary kept driving straight for the gate. When they were only a few feet away, Hannah shouted, "Turn right! Now!"

Mary pulled the reins hard to the right. The horse took a sharp right turn, and the chariot drifted behind kicking dust onto the closed gate.

The High Priest tried to turn, but it was too late. His chariot slid and crashed into the gate.

"Go!" said Hannah.

"Heeyah!" shouted Mary.

The horse headed up a ramp beside the gate that led to the top of the wall surrounding the city. The wall had a road on top of it that was wide enough for two chariots.

"Keep going!" said Hannah.

They followed the road around Babylon. Peter watched the houses and temples whiz by in the city below.

"We're almost home," said Hannah. "Go down that ramp."

Mary tugged the reins and the horse went down the ramp and stopped at the river's edge.

Peter hopped off the chariot.

"That was awesome!" said Peter. Mary and Hannah jumped down after him.

The horse drank from the river. Hank joined it.

"I'm thirsty too," said Peter.

"I wouldn't drink that water if I were you," said Hannah. "We can get some food and drink at my house."

Peter's stomach growled loudly. "Sounds good to me."

They walked down a narrow, dusty street lined with small shops and houses. They came to a shop with a sign written in cuneiform.

"We're home!" said Hannah.

"What does the sign say?" asked Mary.

"Shadrach's Spice Shop," said Hannah.

"You live in a spice shop?" said Peter.

Hannah giggled. "No, this is my grandfather's shop," she said. "My parents are on a journey to find the best spices around the world. So I'm staying here with him."

Mary's eyes got very big. "Your grandfather is Shadrach?"

"Yes," said Hannah. "Have you heard of him?"

Mary wasn't sure how to answer. "The name sounds familiar," she finally answered.

"You've probably heard of him," said Hannah. "People come from everywhere to buy his spices."

Peter gave Mary a look. She almost broke one of the rules.

"Let's go in," said Hannah.

SHADRACH'S TALE

Hannah opened the door, and they entered Shadrach's Spice Shop.

A wave of wonderful scents dazzled Peter's senses. His mouth watered and his stomach growled. Hank ran around the room, smelling the spices and wagging his tail.

An old man with bushy hair and a long white beard stood behind clay pots filled with colorful peppers and cinnamon sticks. "Hello, my beautiful Hannah," he said.

Hannah blushed as she smiled. "Hello,

Grandfather." She gave him a big hug.

"Did you bring friends today?" he said.

"Yes," she said. "They are from a faraway land, and they need to hide."

Shadrach looked at Peter and Mary. "They definitely don't dress like anyone from around here." He hurried to the front door and locked it. "Who are you hiding from?"

"The High Priest," said Mary.

"We wouldn't bow to his idol," said Peter. "So he's trying to catch us and throw us in the dungeon."

Shadrach nodded his head. "It can be hard to take a stand for God," he said. "But trust me, he will protect you."

"Tell them the story," said Hannah.

Shadrach rubbed his long, white beard. "It was many years ago," he said. "King Nebuchadnezzar built a large golden idol. Then he commanded

everyone to bow down
and worship it."

"Tell them
about the fire,"
said Hannah.

"Be patient,"
said Shadrach.
He turned back to
Peter and Mary.
"The king said

that anyone who didn't bow would be thrown
into a fiery furnace!"

"Did you bow?" asked Peter.

Shadrach shook his head. "No," he said, "and
neither did my friends Meshach and Abednego."

"Tell them what happened next!" said Hannah.

"They tied us up and threw us into the raging
fire," said Shadrach. "But God sent an angel to
protect us."

"Tell them about the ropes," said Hannah.

"I was just getting to that," he said. "The ropes burned away, but the fire didn't touch our clothes or any part of our body. God saved us!"

"Was it hot in the fire?" asked Peter. The scroll shook in the bag under Peter's arm.

"It was a little warm," said Shadrach. "But not as hot as my peppers." He grabbed a pepper out of a basket. "Would you like to try one?"

Peter was hungry, but he wanted to see why the scroll shook. "Yes, but can I talk to my sister in private for a minute?" said Peter.

"Of course," said Shadrach.

Peter and Mary walked behind a shelf of spices and unrolled the scroll. The third word glowed and transformed into the word: IN.

"We solved another word," whispered Peter.

"Is everything okay back there?" asked Shadrach.

"Yes," answered Peter. He put the scroll away, and they went back to Shadrach and Hannah. Peter's stomach growled.

"Now, let's find somewhere for you to hide," said Shadrach. "And get you something to eat."

Peter rubbed his belly. "Sounds good to me!"

Shadrach led them through a hidden door in the back of the shop and pointed to a table. "Have a seat."

Peter plopped down on a big pillow beside the table. Mary sat on another.

Shadrach brought in baskets full of bread, apples, juicy grapes, and plums. Then he prayed. "Blessed are you, Lord our God, King of the universe, who brings forth bread from the earth."

"Amen," said Hannah.

"Amen!" said Peter. Then he took a big bite of bread.

They ate until they couldn't eat anymore.

Peter sat back on the pillow and rubbed his full belly. "Thank you," he said. "That was delicious."

Bang! Bang!

Hank ran to the door and growled.

"That's strange," said Shadrach. "The shop is closed, and I'm not expecting any visitors."

"I hope it's not the High Priest," said Mary.

There was another knock at the door.

"Stay here," said Shadrach. "I'll see who it is."

"Be careful," said Hannah.

AN OLD FRIEND

Shadrach shut the door and went into the front of the shop.

Peter pressed his ear against the door and listened.

Bang! Bang!

"I'm coming!" said Shadrach.

Peter held his breath. He hoped it wasn't the High Priest.

"Welcome, old friend!" said Shadrach. "Come in! Come in!"

Mary tapped Peter. "Who is it?"

"I don't know," said Peter. He leaned into the door to hear better.

The door swung open, and Peter tumbled onto the shop floor. He looked up at an old man with bushy, white hair, wise eyes, and a long beard. He wore a purple robe and a chunky, gold  necklace with a medallion of a lion on it. Peter thought he looked like a king.

Peter quickly stood and brushed himself off.

Hank didn't bark—he just sniffed the man's purple robe. The man reached down and petted Hank's head.

"Daniel!" shouted Hannah. She ran over and gave him a big hug.

"Hello, Hannah," said Daniel. "You've grown since I saw you last year."

Hannah twirled around.

"You're as lovely as your mother," said Daniel.

"Thank you," said Hannah.

"Introduce me to your friends," said Daniel.

"This is Peter and his sister, Mary," said Hannah.

"Ruff!" Hank barked and wagged his tail.

"And this is Hank," said Peter as he shook Daniel's hand.

Peter looked over at Mary. Her mouth hung open, but she didn't say a word. She just shook Daniel's hand.

"It's nice to meet you," said Daniel.

"They are believers in the one true God," said Hannah. "And I'm helping them hide."

"Who are they hiding from?" asked Daniel.

"The High Priest of Babylon," said Hannah.

"He tried to make them bow to the idol, but they didn't. So he tried to capture them to throw them into the dungeon."

"The High Priest is causing a lot of problems in Babylon," said Daniel. "He's trying to get everyone to bow to his fake god. And he's trying to get more power with the new king."

"How is the new king?" asked Shadrach. "It looks like he's given you some fancy new clothes."

"It's going well so far," said Daniel. "The king made me one of the top three governors of Babylon."

"Congratulations!" said Shadrach. "You've always been a wise ruler."

"Things aren't perfect though," said Daniel. "The other governors don't like me, and I'm not sure I can trust the new king."

"Why?" said Hannah.

"He throws his enemies in the lions' den!" said Daniel.

"A lions' den? What's that?" said Peter.

Hannah frowned. "It's a deep pit full of hungry lions," she said. "No one comes out of it alive."

Peter's palms began to sweat. "I'll be sure to stay on the king's good side."

"It's nothing to worry about," said Shadrach. "I'm sure God will protect us."

"I'm sure he will," said Daniel.

"What brings you here today, Daniel?" said Shadrach. "Do you need some of my delicious spices?"

"No, I bring news," said Daniel. "God has given me a message. Things are about to change."

Shadrach looked concerned.

"Don't be afraid," said Daniel. "Remember, God has all wisdom and power."

"What's going to happen?" said Hannah.

"Our exile in Babylon will soon come to an end," said Daniel. "And the Israelites will be able to return to Jerusalem."

Shadrach's eyes lit up. "When, Daniel?" said Shadrach. "It's been almost seventy years."

"The time is coming soon," said Daniel.

Shadrach clapped his hands together. "I can't wait to go home!"

"Be patient, Shadrach," Daniel said.

Peter looked at Mary. She gave a small nod. He knew she couldn't wait to go home either.

The sun began to set, and Shadrach lit some candles.

"It's time for me to go," said Daniel.

"Can't you stay a little longer?" said Hannah.

"No," said Daniel. "I need to go home for my evening prayer."

"It was nice meeting you," said Peter.

"I hope we see you again," said Mary.

Daniel looked into Mary's eyes. "You will." Then he looked at Peter. "You don't have to hide. God will protect you."

Daniel hugged Hannah. "See you soon," he said as he was leaving.

Shadrach closed the door. Hannah found some pillows and made a place for Peter, Mary, and Hank to sleep in a back room.

"I'll see you in the morning," said Hannah. Then she shut the door to their room.

Mary and Hank fell asleep in no time. Peter took out the adventure journal and flashlight and wrote.

Day 2

Babylon is an amazing city, but most of the people don't believe in the one true God. Hannah is very kind to help us hide from the High Priest and his annoying raven. Daniel seems very wise. I'm glad he's in charge. I hope we see him again. I'm a little freaked out about the hungry lions. I don't want to be their lunch. I'll just have to trust God to protect us.

Peter closed the journal. He turned off the flashlight and drifted off to sleep.

A Sneaky Plot

Bang! Bang! The knock at the door jolted Peter awake.

"*Woof! Woof!*" Hank barked at the door.

Mary sat straight up in bed. "Oh no, did they find us?" whispered Mary.

Bang! Bang!

Peter stared at the door for a few moments. "I'm not hiding anymore," he said.

"Are you sure?" whispered Mary.

"Yes!" said Peter. "I'm trusting God." He stood up and walked to the door.

He reached out and grabbed the handle. "No more hiding," he whispered to himself. He swung the door open.

"Good morning," Hannah said with a warm smile.

Peter let out a long breath. "I thought you were the High Priest."

"Sorry," said Hannah. "I just wanted to let you know I'm leaving to go and work in the garden."

"Can we go with you?" said Mary.

"Are you sure you don't want to stay here where you're hidden?" said Hannah.

Mary pulled her shoulders back. "No, Peter's right. We need to trust God. We don't need to hide anymore."

Peter smiled. It felt good to be right for once. "Let's go!"

Hank wagged his tail. Peter grabbed the adventure bag, and they headed into the kitchen.

Someone was sitting at the table.

"Daniel!" Hannah ran over to the kitchen table where Daniel was sitting.

"Good morning," said Daniel. "I have a surprise for you!"

Hannah's eyes lit up. "What?"

"I've heard great things about the beautiful work you're doing in the garden," said Daniel.

Hannah's cheeks turned pink. "It's nothing, really."

Shadrach looked proudly at his granddaughter. "She's a hard worker."

Daniel reached into his pocket and pulled out a silver necklace with a sparkling, pink pendant in the shape of a flower. "I've decided to put you in charge of the garden," he said, hanging the necklace around her neck.

"Thank you," said Hannah. "I'll do my best."

"I know you will," said Daniel. "Now let's go to work."

"Can Peter and Mary go with us?" Hannah said hopefully.

"*Woof!*" Hank barked.

Hannah reached down and petted Hank's head. "And Hank too."

"Well, of course," said Daniel. "They can help you in the garden."

Grrrrr! Peter patted his rumbling belly. "Excuse me. I guess I'm a little hungry."

They sat down at the table and ate bananas, berries, and bread before leaving. Shadrach waved as Peter and the others headed down Processional Way to the palace and garden.

After walking for a few minutes, Peter looked to the left and saw the ziggurat rising high against the blue sky. "Maybe we should walk a little bit faster," he said.

"There's nothing to worry about," said Daniel. "I'm in charge of this section of Babylon."

"*Grrrrr!*"

"Is that your stomach growling again?" said Mary. "You can't be hungry already."

"No," said Peter. "It's Hank."

"What's he growling at?" said Hannah.

Peter turned and looked at an open gate leading to the ziggurat.

"*Bow!*" squawked the raven.

The High Priest slowly walked through the gate with the raven sitting on his shoulder. "Well, look who we have here," he snarled. "I told you I would find you."

"We're not hiding anymore," said Peter.

"Fine, have it your way," said the High Priest. "Guards!" he shouted.

The guards rushed out of the gate.

The High Priest pointed at Peter, Mary, and Hank. "Take them to the dungeon!"

"Ruff!" Hank barked and the raven flew away.

Hannah quickly grabbed Daniel's arm. "Do something!"

Daniel stepped in front of them. "You're not taking them anywhere!" he said. "Not while I'm governor!"

The High Priest stared at Daniel's golden necklace. Then he motioned for the guards to step back. "I guess they're safe for now," he said. "But that might not be a problem for long."

"What do you mean?" said Daniel.

"Oh, never mind," said the High Priest.

Roar!

Peter heard lions roaring in the distance.

The High Priest flashed an evil grin. "Sounds like the lions are hungry," he said.

"Let's go," said Daniel, as he turned down Processional Way.

"See you later, Peter and Mary!" shouted the High Priest.

"How does he know your names?" asked Hannah.

"I don't know," said Peter. "But he gives me the creeps."

"Me too," said Daniel.

When they finally made it to the Hanging Gardens, Daniel said goodbye and went to the palace to meet with the king and the other rulers. Peter, Mary, Hannah, and Hank went to work in the garden.

It was hard work in the hot sun. After a few hours, Peter's stomach started growling. "Time for lunch," he said. He rubbed his belly.

They picked bananas and sat in the shade of a large bush. Peter heard footsteps on the other side of the bush. Hank growled.

"*Shhh,*" said Peter. He peeked through the bush and saw the High Priest with two men wearing purple robes and gold necklaces just like Daniel's. Peter quickly sat back.

"Who is it?" whispered Mary.

Peter held his finger up to his lips so that everyone would stay quiet.

"How are things going with the new king?" said the High Priest.

"We have our power back," answered one governor. "But so does Daniel, and he might ruin our plan."

"Why are you so worried about Daniel and his weak God?" said the High Priest.

"The new king loves him," said the second

governor. "And there are rumors that the king is going to make Daniel ruler over all of Babylon."

"We can't have that now, can we?" said the High Priest.

"How can we stop him?" said the first governor.

"We need to get rid of him," snapped the High Priest.

"How?" asked the other governor.

"We'll get the king to do it," said the High Priest.

"But he loves Daniel," said the first governor, "and Daniel never does anything wrong."

"Daniel has a weakness," said the High Priest. "He is stubborn and will not worship or pray to any god but his own."

"What's your plan?" said the governor.

"We'll have the king make a law that no one can pray to any god or man but him for the next thirty days," said the High Priest. "Or they will be thrown into the pit full of hungry lions!"

"That's genius," said the other governor.

"Yes, it is," said the High Priest. "Now go and meet with the king and the other rulers!"

Peter heard the men leave.

"This is terrible!" said Hannah. "We have to warn Daniel!"

Daniel in Danger

They ran to the palace to find Daniel. It was huge and decorated in shimmering blue and yellow tiles. It was surrounded by palm trees and soldiers.

"Will they let us in?" said Mary.

"I hope so," said Hannah.

At the door, soldiers stood guard with round shields, sharp swords, and long spears.

"Excuse me," said Hannah.

One of the guards looked down. "What do you want?" he said in a gruff voice.

"I need to see Daniel," she said.

"No one can enter the palace," the guard said.

"Why?" asked Hannah.

"The king is having a very important meeting with the governors and leaders of Babylon," said the guard.

"But I have to see him now," said Hannah.

"It's a matter of life and death!" said Peter.

"You'll have to wait until after the meeting," said the guard, turning away.

So they waited and waited. Finally, the door swung open, and the leaders streamed out. Peter watched as the important people walked by, but he didn't see Daniel. The last to walk out were the two governors in purple robes.

"We've got Daniel now," said one of the governors as they walked past.

"You can go in now," said the guard.

Peter, Mary, Hannah, and Hank searched and searched but couldn't find Daniel anywhere.

"*Woof!*" Hank barked and sniffed a colorful rug in the middle of a huge room surrounded by paintings of chariots, horses, and kings.

"What is it Hank?" said Peter. "Do you smell Daniel?"

"*Woof!*" Hank barked and wagged his tail.

"Find Daniel," said Peter. Hank put his nose to the ground and began tracking.

Peter, Mary, and Hannah followed Hank out of the palace, past the garden, and across the street. Hank stopped in front of a huge house and barked.

It was larger than most of the houses in Babylon, with two stories and a wooden door.

"This is Daniel's house!" said Hannah. "I remember visiting last year with my parents."

Mary knocked.

The door swung open. "Come in," said Daniel.

Hannah told Daniel about the governors' plot.

Daniel held up a scroll with a purple wax seal. "It's true," he said. "The king signed the law."

"What will you do?" asked Peter.

Daniel walked over and looked out the window as the sun began to set. "God will protect me," he said.

Daniel turned and placed the scroll on a table. "It's getting late," he said. "You can sleep here tonight. I have plenty of rooms."

Daniel headed up the stairs. He pointed Hannah into one room, and Peter, Mary, and Hank into a room across the hall.

"My room is right next door if you need anything," Daniel said as he closed the door.

Peter went over and pressed his ear against the wall.

"What is he doing?" said Mary.

"He's praying."

Hank ran over to the window and barked.

Peter looked out the second-story window and saw the two governors and the High Priest on the street below.

"We caught him," said the High Priest. "Now, let's go tell the king."

The governors nodded. They turned and walked down the dark street toward the palace.

Peter and Mary ran across the hall and told Hannah what happened.

Hannah knocked on Daniel's door and told him.

"I know," said Daniel. "I saw them too."

Tears ran down Hannah cheeks. "Why did you do it?"

Daniel reached down and wiped away a tear. "Follow me. I have something to show you."

Daniel led them down the long hallway. They climbed a set of stairs and went through a small passageway to the roof. Peter thought the roof looked like a big patio. He could see the whole city.

"It's beautiful up here," said Mary.

"What do you want to show us?" said Peter.

"I want to show you why I pray and worship God," he said. Daniel pointed toward the star-filled sky. "God is amazing! He is so powerful that he spoke and created everything in the universe."

Peter stared into the night sky. He remembered hearing God speak and seeing the sun, moon, and stars appear out of empty darkness.

Daniel pointed at the temples scattered across Babylon. "Those temples are filled with fake gods," he said. "They are made of wood and stone. They can't hear or speak. The people of Babylon are worshiping idols they have created, and not the God who created everything."

Peter shook his head. He remembered how cold and creepy the idol of Marduk was.

"I worship God because He is good and loves us," said Daniel. He took a deep breath. "God gave us the breath of life and takes care of us."

Daniel put his arm around Hannah's shoulders. "Even when life is confusing and scary, remember that God is with you and loves you always."

Hannah smiled. "I'll remember."

Then Daniel pointed to the palace. "The king isn't in control," he said. "God is in control. Kings and kingdoms will come and go."

Daniel looked back toward the starry sky. "One day, the Great One will come. He will be the Great King, and all the people on earth will live in peace and joy. His kingdom will last forever."

"God *is* amazing," Peter said. He looked deep into the night sky. He knew he would worship only the one true God. Peter looked over at Mary and Hannah. Their eyes were shining as they looked out at the stars too.

After a few more quiet moments, Daniel took them back downstairs to their rooms.

Hank curled up on a pillow and started snoring. Mary closed her eyes and was soon asleep on a mat on the floor.

Peter tossed and turned on his mat. His mind filled with worry. *What if the lions eat Daniel? What if we get thrown to the hungry lions with Daniel? What if we can't solve the scroll? What if we never get to see our parents again?*

Peter knew that he should trust God, but sometimes it was hard. So Peter prayed in a whisper, "Dear God, please protect Daniel and help us solve the secret of the scroll. Please give me strength and peace. I will trust in you. Amen."

12

INTO THE LIONS' DEN

The morning sunlight crept through the window and woke Peter. He rubbed the sleep out of his eyes. He sat up and saw Mary staring at the unrolled scroll.

"Have you figured it out?" he asked.

Mary sighed and shook her head. "Why is it so hard?"

Just then, the scroll shook, and the second word glowed and transformed into the word: IS.

"You did it, Mary!" shouted Peter. "Only one word left!"

Mary picked up the scroll and read, "God is in _____."

"What is God in?" said Peter.

Knock! Knock!

Mary quickly shoved the scroll in the adventure bag as Peter opened the door.

"Good morning," said Hannah.

"Have they taken Daniel to the lions' den?" asked Peter.

"No," she said. "He's downstairs making breakfast."

Peter and Mary followed Hannah down to the kitchen. Peter's mouth watered when he saw the table covered with fruit, bread, and cheese. Hank sniffed at the air and wagged his tail.

"Good morning," said Daniel. "Would you like something to eat?"

"Yes, please," said Peter, plopping down on a pillow beside the table.

Daniel prayed and thanked God for the food. Then they all ate.

"I hope this isn't your last meal, Daniel," said Peter.

Mary gave him *the look*. "You shouldn't say things like that," she said in a stern voice.

"Well, it's true," said Peter.

"It's okay," said Daniel. "I hope so too, but I trust God."

"Maybe the king has changed his mind," said Hannah. "Maybe he won't throw you in the lions' den."

Daniel shook his head sadly. "He can't," he said. "Once the king makes a law, it cannot be changed."

"What do we do?" said Hannah.

"We wait," said Daniel.

So that's what they did. They spent the day at Daniel's house, and they waited and waited and waited.

Hours later, Peter looked out the back window and saw the sun beginning to lower in the sky. "Maybe the king changed his mind," he said. "Maybe you're not going to be thrown into the lions' den."

Bang! Bang! Peter froze.

Daniel opened the door. Soldiers carrying shields and swords shoved their way into the house. The two governors stood behind the soldiers.

"There's the law breaker!" one of the governors shouted. "Arrest him!"

The soldiers surrounded Daniel and tied his hands behind his back.

"No!" Hannah sobbed. "You can't throw him to the lions."

Mary put her arm around Hannah.

"Yes, we can!" said the governor. "Maybe we should arrest you kids too."

Peter gulped. Hank crouched in front of them and growled.

"No," said Daniel. "Leave them alone. It's me you're after."

"Take him away!" said the governor. The soldiers led Daniel out of his house.

"What should we do?" said Mary.

"Let's follow them," said Peter, "and see where they take him."

They followed Daniel and the soldiers down Processional Way. They walked past the palace to the Ishtar Gate.

"Bow!"

Peter turned and saw the raven perched on the High Priest's shoulder.

Roar!

The lions' roars came from outside the open gate.

"The lions sound hungry today," said the High Priest. "I wouldn't get too close if I were you."

Peter turned toward the High Priest.

"Just ignore him," said Mary.

They walked past the High Priest and followed

Daniel and the soldiers outside of Babylon and up a small, sandy hill.

"There's the king," said Hannah. "He looks so sad."

Ahead, Peter saw the king standing on top of the hill next to a big hole.

Roar! Roar! The sounds of the hungry lions echoed out of the hole. The sun set lower and the sky grew darker.

The soldiers led Daniel to the king. The governors and the other leaders gathered around. Peter peeked between a couple of men so he could see.

The king looked into Daniel's eyes and said, "May your God, whom you faithfully serve, rescue you." Then he lowered his head and sighed. "Throw him in the lions' den."

The soldiers shoved Daniel into the hole.

Peter heard the lions roaring and snarling as

soldiers shoved a large rock over the top of the entrance to the den. Another soldier poured melted purple wax on top of the rock. The king pressed his seal into the wax using his ring and walked away. Then the governors and leaders did the same.

"His fate is sealed," said one of the governors as he walked past Peter.

The other governor smiled. "We'll see if his God can protect him."

"God will protect him!" shouted Peter.

The governors looked at Peter and laughed as they walked away.

Peter heard muffled roars coming from the den.

Hannah held her hands over her ears, "I can't take it anymore," she sobbed.

"Let's go," said Peter. "There's nothing we can do."

THE FINAL FACE-OFF

Peter and Hank took off down the street. Peter looked back at Mary and Hannah. "Come on!"

They were out of breath when they finally got to Shadrach's Spice Shop.

Shadrach opened the door as they approached. "What happened?"

"They arrested Daniel and threw him in the lions' den!" said Hannah. "It was horrible . . . just horrible."

"Why did the governors arrest Daniel?" asked Shadrach.

Hannah told him about the sneaky plot by the governors and the High Priest.

"What should we do?" said Mary.

"There is only one thing we can do," said Shadrach. "Pray that God protects Daniel."

Hannah paced. "If we pray, we might be thrown to the lions too."

"God is more powerful than any law or king," said Shadrach. "We must trust that God will protect us."

Shadrach looked out into the dark night. "It's late," he said. "Go to your rooms and pray."

When Peter shut the bedroom door, he turned to Mary. "Let's go back and see if Daniel's okay."

"We can't," said Mary. "We need to solve the secret of the scroll before the sun rises. Or we'll be stuck here."

"Maybe there's a clue at the lions' den," said Peter.

"I guess . . . ," said Mary. "Okay, let's go."

Hank leaped out of the window. Peter and Mary climbed out more carefully, and they made their way down the dark, quiet streets of Babylon. They walked past the palace and through the Ishtar Gate.

Hank ran ahead and barked at the large rock covering the entrance to the pit full of lions—and Daniel.

Peter tried to shove the huge rock away from the hole in the ground, but it wouldn't budge. Mary joined in. They huffed and puffed and pushed, but they couldn't move the rock.

"What do we do now?" said Peter.

"I guess we pray," said Mary.

Peter got down on his knees. "Dear Lord, please help Daniel."

"*Woof! Woof!*"

Peter looked up as the raven landed on top of the big rock.

Hank growled at the darkness behind them.

"Well, well, look what we have here," said the High Priest. "Some more law breakers."

Peter jumped to his feet. "We were just trying to see if Daniel was okay."

"You're too late!" snarled the High Priest. "The lions have eaten him by now."

"No," said Peter. "God will protect him."

The High Priest laughed. "God won't protect Daniel," he said. "And I know he won't protect you this time."

"What do you mean by 'this time'?" said Mary.

The raven flew over and perched on the High Priest's shoulder.

"You kids keep showing up and wrecking my plans. First it was in the garden, then at the ark and in Egypt and Jericho and Bethlehem," said the High Priest. "But now I've got you!"

Peter looked into his cold, dark eyes. "We should have know it was you, Satan."

The High Priest slowly clapped his hands. "You finally figured it out," he said. "But it's too late! Daniel is out of the way. Now I can become the ruler of Babylon and then the whole world."

"Bow!" squawked the raven.

"Yes," said the High Priest. "Everyone will bow to me, and I will be in control of everything."

"Your plan won't work," said Peter. "God is in control." He felt the scroll shaking in the adventure bag.

"You're wrong," said the High Priest. "Daniel is dead, and no one can stop me."

"No," said Mary. "I know Daniel is still alive."

"Are you sure?" said the High Priest. He slowly walked around them and shoved the huge rock away. Peter was surprised how strong he was.

Roar! Roar! The sound of angry lions echoed out of the den.

Hank growled at the edge of the pit.

"Look for yourselves," said the High Priest.

Peter and Mary edged closer. Peter's heart pounded as he squinted into the dark pit. He couldn't see anything.

"Take a closer look," said the High Priest.

A Song of Safety

Peter and Mary crawled closer to get a better look. Then the High Priest shoved them from behind. Peter, Mary, and Hank tumbled into the pit.

Roar!

Mary jumped up and wiped the dust off her pants. "Let's get out of here!"

They tried to climb up the slippery, rocky walls, but the High Priest shoved the rock back over the hole. It was completely dark.

The lions roared through the darkness. Then a bright light appeared on the other side of the pit.

Peter looked and saw Michael spreading his mighty wings and holding his glowing sword.

"Hurry!" shouted Michael. "Get behind me!"

Peter, Mary, and Hank quickly scooted around the rocky edge of the pit. The lions snapped at their heels as they dove behind Michael.

There was Daniel—without a scratch!

"You're alive!" said Mary.

"Of course I am," said Daniel. "I told you God would protect me."

Peter peeked around Michael and saw the lions pacing back and forth.

"It's getting late," said Michael, "I think everyone should get some rest."

"How can we sleep with those lions waiting to pounce on us!" said Peter.

"Leave that to me," said Michael. Then he began to sing.

It was the most beautiful song Peter had ever

heard. The lions yawned. Then they curled up on the rocks and fell asleep. Peter heard Daniel snoring behind him.

Mary rubbed her eyes. "That was a wonderful song," she said. "Can you sing it again?"

"Not right now," said Michael. "You need to solve the secret of the scroll before the sun rises."

Peter shook his body to stay awake. "Oh yeah," he whispered. "I almost forgot. It shook outside."

He took the scroll out of the bag and unrolled it. The final word glowed and transformed into the word: CONTROL.

Peter read the scroll, "GOD IS IN CONTROL."

Michael smiled. "Yes, he is."

Peter grabbed Mary's hand. Mary bent down and hugged Hank.

The lions' den rumbled and crumbled around them. And they were back safe and sound in Great-Uncle Solomon's library.

Peter looked down at the scroll in his hand. The red wax seal transformed into a gold medallion and fell to the floor. Peter picked it up and looked at the inscription of a lion. It looked just like the one on Daniel's necklace.

Great-Uncle Solomon rushed into the library. "You're back! Was it another amazing adventure?"

Mary told him about the ziggurat, the evil

High Priest, and his
annoying raven.
Peter told him
how they escaped
on a chariot. Mary
described meeting
Hannah in the beautiful
Hanging Gardens of Babylon.

"I would have loved to see those gardens,"
said Great-Uncle Solomon.

Then Peter told him about the plot to throw
Daniel in the lions' den and how God sent
Michael to protect them.

"I hope Daniel made it out okay," said Peter.

Great-Uncle Solomon went to a shelf and
pulled out his big, red Bible. "Let me tell you the
rest of the story."

He told them how Daniel survived without
a scratch and how the king was very impressed

with Daniel and God. The king made Daniel a great ruler and decided to let the Israelites return to Jerusalem and rebuild the Temple.

Mary smiled. "I know that made Hannah and Shadrach happy," she said.

"The Israelites were glad to return to their home," said Great-Uncle Solomon, "But they still were looking forward to the Great King to come and bring peace."

"Tell us about the Great King," said Peter.

Great-Uncle Solomon put his Bible back on the shelf. "That is a story for another day."

"We found something in Babylon you have to see!" said Peter. "Follow me."

Peter led them out of the library and back to the room with the lion statue. He dug into his adventure bag and pulled out the tiles.

Mary slid the tiles into place and completed the puzzle of the lion.

Great-Uncle Solomon clapped his hands. "You did it!" he said. "You solved the puzzle."

Peter looked at the gold medallion in his hand. He couldn't wait to hear the lion roar again.

Do you want to read more about the events in this story?

The people, places, and events in *The Lion's Roar* are drawn from the stories in the Bible. You can read more about them in the following passages in the Bible.

Daniel chapter 1 tells the story of young Daniel and many other Israelites being captured and taken to live in Babylon.

Daniel chapter 3 tells about Shadrach, Meshach, and Abednego refusing to bow to an idol and being thrown into a fiery furnace.

Daniel 6:1-15 tells about Daniel becoming a governor in Babylon and the plot against him.

Daniel 6:16-28 tells the story of Daniel being thrown into the lions' den.

Special Note:
Hannah is a fictional character representing the Jewish children living in Babylon during the time of the Israelites' exile from Jerusalem.

CATCH ALL
PETER AND MARY'S ADVENTURES!

In *The Beginning*, Peter, Mary, and Hank witness the Creation of the earth while battling a sneaky snake.

In *Race to the Ark*, the trio must rush to help Noah finish the ark before the coming flood.

In *The Great Escape*, Peter, Mary, and Hank journey to Egypt and see the devastation of the plagues.

In *Journey to Jericho*, the trio lands in Jericho as the Israelites prepare to enter the Promised Land.

In **The Shepherd's Stone**, Peter, Mary, and Hank accompany David as he prepares to fight Goliath.

In **The Lion's Roar**, the trio arrive in Babylon and uncover a secret plot to get Daniel thrown in the lions' den.

In **The King Is Born**, Peter, Mary, and Hank visit Bethlehem at the time of Jesus' birth.

In *Miracles by the Sea*, the trio meets Jesus and the disciples and witnesses amazing miracles.

In **The Final Scroll**, Peter, Mary, and Hank travel back to Jerusalem and witness Jesus' crucifixion and resurrection.

ABOUT THE AUTHOR

 Mike Thomas grew up in Florida playing sports and riding his bike to the library and the arcade. He graduated from Liberty University, where he earned a bachelor's degree in Bible Studies.

When his son Peter was nine years old, Mike went searching for books that would teach Peter about the Bible in a fun and imaginative way. Finding none, he decided to write his own series. In The Secret of the Hidden Scrolls, Mike combines biblical accuracy with adventure, imagination, and characters who are dear to his heart. The main characters are named after Mike's son Peter, his niece Mary, and his dog, Hank.

Mike Thomas lives in Tennessee with his wife, Lori; two sons, Payton and Peter; and Hank.

For more information about the author and the series, visit www.secretofthehiddenscrolls.com.